Always Room for More

by Paul Webb
illustrated by Dee Texidor

Harcourt
SCHOOL PUBLISHERS

Copyright © by Harcourt, Inc.

All rights reserved. No part of this publication may be reproduced or transmitted in any form or by any means, electronic or mechanical, including photocopy, recording, or any information storage and retrieval system, without permission in writing from the publisher.

Requests for permission to make copies of any part of the work should be addressed to School Permissions and Copyrights, Harcourt, Inc., 6277 Sea Harbor Drive, Orlando, Florida 32887–6777. Fax: 407-345-2418.

HARCOURT and the Harcourt Logo are trademarks of Harcourt, Inc., registered in the United States of America and/or other jurisdictions.

Printed in China

ISBN 10: 0-15-350619-9
ISBN 13: 978-0-15-350619-2

Ordering Options
ISBN 10: 0-15-350598-2 (Grade 1 On-Level Collection)
ISBN 13: 978-0-15-350598-0 (Grade 1 On-Level Collection)
ISBN 10: 0-15-357774-6 (package of 5)
ISBN 13: 978-0-15-357774-1 (package of 5)

If you have received these materials as examination copies free of charge, Harcourt School Publishers retains title to the materials and they may not be resold. Resale of examination copies is strictly prohibited and is illegal.

Possession of this publication in print format does not entitle users to convert this publication, or any portion of it, into electronic format.

5 6 7 8 9 10   468   15 14 13 12 11 10 09

A little starling saw the first stars of the night. "I know a nice cow that lives here," she said. "I'll stop at Cow's barn for the night."

Then Robin came. "Can I please sit by you?" he asked.

"Join me," said Starling. "There is always room for more."

Robin hopped onto the branch.

Soon Lark came flying by. "Can I please sit by you?" called Lark.

"Yes, come join us," said Robin. "There is always room for more."

When it was getting
very dark, Stork came.
"Can I please sit by you?"
asked Stork.

"Join us," Lark said to
her. "There is always room
for more."

Crash! Down they all
went!

Cow called out loud,
"Are you hurt?"

"No," said the birds.

"Join me," said Cow.
"There is room for all of
you in the barn."

"Thank you very much!"
This time, Starling sat
by Cow.

Robin sat by Starling.
Lark sat by Robin.
Stork sat by Lark.

All the animals slept
well in Cow's barn.